MARC BROWN

ARTHUR'S BABY

SCHOLASTIC INC.
New York Toronto London Auckland Sydney

◇FOR TOLON, TUCKER AND ELIZA◇
my three babies

ISBN 0-590-63477-1

Copyright © 1987 by Marc Brown. All rights reserved. Published by Scholastic Inc., 555 Broadway, New York, NY 10012, by arrangement with Little, Brown and Company (Inc.)

SCHOLASTIC and associated logos are trademarks and/or registered trademarks of Scholastic Inc.

12 11 10 9 8 7 6 5 4 3 2 1   8 9/9 0 1 2 3/0

Printed in the U.S.A.   09

"We have a surprise for you," said Mother and Father.
"Is it a bicycle?" asked Arthur.

"We're going to have a baby!" said Mother.
"Ooooo," squealed D.W. "I love babies!"
"A *baby*?" said Arthur.
"Yes, in about six months," said Father.
"Plenty of time for us all to get ready."

Arthur's friends had lots of advice.
"Better get some earplugs," said Binky Barnes,
"or you'll never sleep."

"Forget about playing after school," said Buster.
"You'll have to babysit."

"You'll have to change all those dirty diapers!"
said Muffy.

"And you'll probably start talking baby talk,"
said Francine. "Doo doo ga ga boo boo."

For the next few months, everywhere
Arthur looked there were babies — more
and more babies.
"I think babies are taking over the world!"
said Arthur.

"Don't look now," said Buster,
"but you could be in for triple trouble."

One day after school, D.W. grabbed
Arthur's arm.
"I will teach you how to diaper a baby," she said.
"Don't worry about diapers," said Mother.
"Come sit next to me. I want to show you
something."

Arthur age 9 months

"Is that really me?" asked Arthur.
"Yes," said Mother. "You were such a cute baby."

Arthur age 1 year

D.W. age 2 months

"Look," said D.W. "This is me with Mommy and Daddy. Don't I look adorable?"

D.W. age 5 months

That Saturday morning, Mother took out her suitcase.

"Where are you going?" asked Arthur.

"The baby could come any day now," said Mother.

"I need to be ready for the hospital."

"Here," said D.W. "Something for you to look at while you're there."

Sunday morning, Arthur and D.W. found
Grandma Thora fixing breakfast.
"You have a new sister!" she said.
"Yippee! Yippee! Yippee!" said D.W. "She'll be
just like me!"
"That's what I'm afraid of," said Arthur.

The next day, they went to the hospital to see
the new baby.

"We named her Kate," said Father.

"I think she has your nose, Arthur."

"I think she has D.W.'s mouth," said Arthur.

On Tuesday, Mother and Father brought Kate home.
Everyone was acting like they'd never seen
a baby before.
Every time the doorbell rang, more presents arrived.
"They're not for you, Arthur," said D.W.
"They're for the baby."

"Arthur, don't you want to try holding Kate?"
Mother asked.
"Can I have another turn first?" asked D.W.
"It's Arthur's turn," Mother said.
"I'd rather look," said Arthur.
"It's just as well," said D.W.
"Arthur doesn't know beans
about babies."

A few days later, Mother needed some help.
"I have to go upstairs," she said. "Arthur, would
you watch Kate?"
"*Me?*" asked Arthur. "What do I do?"
"Don't worry," said D.W. "I'll take care
of everything."

When the doorbell rang, D.W. answered the door.
"Arthur can't play," she said. "He has to babysit.
But you can come in and see my baby."

"Don't get too close, because you all have germs!
And be quiet," D.W. said, "my baby is sleeping."

"Look!" said Francine. "She opened her eyes."
"Stand back," said D.W. "She wants her bottle."

Kate drank her bottle in a flash.

Then she began to cry.
"Everyone remain calm," said D.W.

D.W. gave Kate a kiss.
Kate cried louder.

D.W. bounced Kate.
Kate screamed.

"Arthur, quick! Do something!" D.W. said.
"She's your baby, too."
"All of a sudden she's *my* baby," said Arthur.
"Why is she crying?" asked D.W.
"She's trying to tell you something," said Arthur.
"What?" asked D.W.
"Listen carefully," said Arthur.

"Burp!" said Kate.
"Is everything all right?" asked Mother.
"It is now," Arthur answered.